This fun **Phonics** reader

belongs to

_____

Ladybird Reading
Phonics
BOOK 5

Contents

A catalogue record for this book is available from the British Library

Published by Ladybird Books Ltd
80 Strand London WC2R 0RL
A Penguin Company

2 4 6 8 10 9 7 5 3 1
© LADYBIRD BOOKS LTD MMVI
LADYBIRD and the device of a Ladybird are trademarks of Ladybird Books Ltd

ISBN-13: 978-1-84646-317-4
ISBN-10: 1-84646-317-3

Printed in Italy

Sheriff Showoff

by Clive Gifford
illustrated by Spike Gerrell

The best
in
the West

introducing the **ff** and **st**
letter groups, as in sniff and best

Big Bad Wolf came into the store. The storekeeper was scared stiff.

"I'll huff and I'll puff, then I'll steal all your stuff," said Big Bad Wolf.

Sheriff Showoff was
riding past.

"With my star on my chest,
I'm the best in the West,"
said Sheriff Showoff.

Big Bad Wolf just sniffed.

"I'll huff and I'll puff, then I'll knock your star off," he said.

There was a scuffle in the dust.

GET OFF!

Wolf ran off.

Sheriff Showoff was left in
handcuffs, with his hat
in the dust.

Up Jumped Mr Crump

by Clive Gifford
illustrated by Karl Richardson

introducing the **mp**, **lp** and **nch**
sounds, as in jump, help and pinch

Mr Crump jumped up.

"Help!" he yelped. "The Bogie Bunch are here. They've come to gobble us up for lunch!

They will pinch us and punch us!

They will crunch us and munch us!

They will jump on us and romp on us!

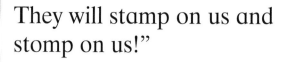
They will stamp on us and stomp on us!"

Mrs Crump put on the lamp.

"You silly old lump," she said to Mr Crump. "It's just Scamp and Plump."

All Mr Crump said was,
"Humph!"

Handstand Andy and Bendy Wendy

by Richard Dungworth
illustrated by Becky Cole

introducing the **nd** and **fl** sounds,
as in bend and flap

This is my friend Andy and his little sister Wendy.

As you can see, the two of
them are very, very bendy.

Wendy spends the weekend
jumping till she flops.

She flips and she flaps, again and again, then falls down flat and stops.

Wendy's brother Andy likes handstands best of all.

He does them on the bandstand,

in the grandstand,

or up against
a wall.

I'm sure that you would find it strange to see us all out shopping,

with Andy standing on his hands, and Wendy flip-flap-flopping.

HOW TO USE
Phonics
BOOK 5

This book introduces your child to common 'consonant blends' – combinations of two or more consonant sounds, such as fl in the word 'flip', or st in the word 'just'. The fun stories will help your child to begin reading simple words containing these common blends.

- Read each story through to your child first. Familiarity helps children to identify some of the words and phrases.

- Have fun talking about the sounds and pictures together – what repeated sounds can your child hear in each story?

- Break new words into separate sounds (eg: h-a-nd) and blend their sounds together to say the word.

- Point out how words with the same written ending often rhyme. If b-est says 'best', what does r-est or ch-est say?

- Some common words, such as 'would', 'said' and even 'the', can't be read by sounding out. Help your child to practise recognising words like these.

Phonic fun

Playing word games is a fun way to build phonic skills. Write down a consonant group and see how many words your child can think of beginning or ending with that group. For extra fun, try making up silly sentences together, using some or all of the words.

Flo flung the flan flat on the floor, with a flop.

Ladybird Reading

Phonics

Phonics is part of the Ladybird Reading range. It can be used alongside any other reading programme, and is an ideal way to practise the reading work that your child is doing, or about to do in school.

Ladybird has been a leading publisher of reading programmes for the last fifty years. **Phonics** combines this experience with the latest research to provide a rapid route to reading success.

The fresh quirky stories in Ladybird's twelve **Phonics** storybooks are designed to help your child have fun learning the relationship between letters, or groups of letters, and the sounds they represent.

This is an important step towards independent reading – it will enable your child to tackle new words by sounding out and blending their separate parts.

The best
in
the West

How Phonics works

- The stories and rhymes introduce the most common spellings of over 40 key sounds, known as phonemes, in a step-by-step way.

- Rhyme and alliteration (the repetition of an initial sound) help to emphasise new sounds.

- Bright amusing illustrations provide helpful picture clues and extra appeal.